One Swell Dad

To ———————————————————————

From ———————————————————————

PAPA: A fond name for father, used in many languages.

FATHERLY: Paternal; like a father; tender; protecting; careful.

FATHERLINESS: The tenderness of a father; paternal kindness.

—Samuel Johnson
A Dictionary of the English Language
1775

One Swell Dad

The Sweet Nellie Book of

Memories and Expressions of

Fatherly Endearment from the Past

PAT ROSS

VIKING STUDIO BOOKS

VIKING STUDIO BOOKS
Published by the Penguin Group
Viking Penguin, a division of Penguin Books USA, Inc.,
375 Hudson Street, New York, New York 10014, U.S.A.
Penguin Books Ltd, 27 Wrights Lane, London W8 5TZ, England
Penguin Books Australia Ltd, Ringwood, Victoria, Australia
Penguin Books Canada Ltd, 10 Alcorn Avenue, Suite 300, Toronto, Ontario, Canada M4V 3B2
Penguin Books (N.Z.) Ltd, 182-190 Wairau Road, Auckland 10, New Zealand

Penguin Books Ltd, Registered Offices: Harmondsworth, Middlesex, England

First published in 1992 by Viking Penguin, a division of Penguin Books USA Inc.

1   3   5   7   9   10   8   6   4   2

"The Four Seasons of Life: Middle Age–'The Season of Strength'"
by Currier & Ives (page 14) and "Martineau: The Last Day in the Old Home"
by Robert Braithwaite (page 42) are reproduced courtesy of
The Granger Collection, New York, New York.

CIP data available.

Printed in Singapore   Set in Nicholas Cochin   Designed by Amy Hill

AN APPRECIATION

The publication of my book *Motherly Devotion* brought praise from many men who were happy to find a small gift for a mother, daughter, sister, or friend. But it also brought hints of discontent. Michael Fragnito, publisher of Viking Studio Books, was the first to let us know that he felt left out. A father of three now, he was ready for some old-fashioned praise. Leisa Crane, who has been my steady companion in researching all the books, said that "Dad, John [her brother], and Charlie [her husband]—my swell guys—were waiting for their book." My husband, Joel, felt a twinge of discrimination.

So this page of appreciation is mostly for the men in our lives—particularly the men at Penguin USA and the many men behind the women who make these small books possible. You know who you are. And this meaningful token is for you, with affection!

INTRODUCTION

Most of us are fortunate enough to have more than one "swell dad" in our lives. Fathers are, of course, at the top of the list, along with their own fathers, and, if we are so lucky, their fathers. The number of dads we know multiplies in a happy geometric progression—to include brothers, sons, uncles, close friends, and beyond. Thoughts of these special men bring memories of times present and times past.

I thought of my own grandfather many times as I searched for excerpts about grandfathers, who go largely unmentioned in nineteenth-century literature, undoubtedly because their lives were, sadly, shorter than they are today. I always took my grandfather, called "Pop Hooper" by both his friends and family, for granted. His warm, accepting way never required more. A short round fellow whose bald spot shone like a new apple, he never failed to stop at his favorite bakery in Baltimore to bring my favorite sticky buns on his frequent visits. A parsimonious man, Pop relished saving money on things like dented canned goods and two-day-old bagels, yet he insisted on buying my sister and me "the best" school shoes every fall. We grew up with strong arches, thinking all bagels could break windows.

When I was sixteen, a boy broke my heart and I took to my room, promptly sinking into tearful self-pity all weekend. I remember hearing Pop's hesitant footsteps, a sort of fat man's shuffle, outside my bedroom door, then his helpless knock. Given to theatrics, I never missed a sob. Pop didn't say a word. He simply patted my head sympathetically, then left as quietly as he had entered. Pop died nearly twenty years ago. I've long forgotten the boy's name, but I still feel Pop's comforting touch as though it were yesterday.

It seems appropriate to mention something here about Father's Day and its history; however, my encyclopedia offers no listing. The Mother's Day entry contains much detail, Valentine's Day is complete, even Arbor Day has been given a few lines. Yet Father's Day is unsung. Perhaps it is enough that we remember our "swell dads" now and all year 'round.

Fatherhood

I would write a book on the duties of fatherhood if I thought the men would read it, but they wouldn't. Good fathers wouldn't need it, and as for bad ones . . .

—*The Ideas of a Plain Country Woman*
1908

Though the father must be a hero . . . he must not be a statue.

—Samuel S. Drury
Fathers and Sons
c. 1927

It is a wise father that knows his own child.

—William Shakespeare
The Merchant of Venice
1600

Wise is the child that knows its sire,
The ancient proverb ran;
But wiser far the man who knows
How, when and where his offspring grows.

—Rudyard Kipling
My Sons in Michigan
c. 1897

Grandfathers should always live long enough to dramatize their old age for their grandchildren in lovable and understandable form. Children so favored receive an impression that does not desert them soon.

—Frances Lester Warner
The Unintentional Charm of Men
1928

Let us now praise famous men, and our fathers that begat us.

—Ecclesiastes XLIV:1

It is the family's expectation that will make father into his best and biggest self.

A man's best investment being his family, his most pressing business is suitably to bring up, to share in bringing up, his children.

—Samuel S. Drury
Fathers and Sons
c. 1927

Father should be neither seen nor heard. That is the only proper basis for family life.

—Oscar Wilde
An Ideal Husband
1895

My hands are too tired to hold a torch on high, but they can light a candle in a nursery. I think all my hopes and ambitions are to be realized in the boy.

—Ellis Meredith
Heart of My Heart

Proud
New Papas

THE
FOND
PAPA

Nothing in literature prepares a father for his role. Motherhood is swamped with books—poetic, fictional, factual. No authority discourses on the prenatal and postpartum care of young fathers.

Fatherhood, for me, has been less a job than an unstable and surprising combination of adventure, blindman's bluff, guerrilla warfare and crossword puzzle.

—Frederic F. Van de Water
Fathers are Funny
1939

The character and history
of each child may be a new
and poetic experience to the
parent, if he will let it.

—Margaret Fuller
Summer on the Lakes
1844

But your new baby has come to stay. It is well for you to know in
advance that he will sometimes be troublesome and annoying. . . .
All this means is that even the best of good fathers, in spite of loving
their children, are quite humanly often inconvenienced and annoyed
by them.

—O. *S*purgeon English, M.D., and
Constance J. Foster
*Fathers Are Parents, T*oo
c. 1951

The father who holds the baby only when it is sweet and fresh; who plays on the nursery floor when things go along like a song; who gingerly tiptoes away at times of tears or disciplinary show-downs, is just a dilettante papa, with a touch of the coward, and not a complete father.

—Samuel S. Drury
Fathers and Sons
c. 1927

But though numerically the mother's duties are five to one with the father's, the paternal responsibility is as heavy as the maternal.

—Samuel S. Drury
Fathers and Sons
c. 1927

When I had determined that your uproar was not due to physical discomfort but instead was merely literary comment, I would strive to quiet you with lullabies. To no one else, before or since, has my singing voice been soothing, but you evidently approved of it.

—Frederic F. Van de Water
Fathers are Funny
1939

Father, father, where are you going?
O do not walk so fast.
Speak, father, speak to your little boy
Or else I shall be lost.

—William Blake
Songs of Innocence: "The Little Boy Lost"
1789

Their Own Boyhoods

There comes a time in every rightly constructed boy's life when he has a raging desire to go somewhere and dig for hidden treasure.

—Attributed to Mark Twain

William J. Bray

A boy's will is the wind's will.
And the thoughts of youth are long, long thoughts.

—Henry Wadsworth Longfellow
"My Lost Youth"
1855

Above all things, as a child, he should have tumbled about in a library.

—Oliver Wendell Holmes
The Autocrat at the Breakfast Table
1858

Oh, for boyhood's painless play,
Sleep that wakes in laughing day,
Health that mocks the doctor's rules,
Knowledge never learned of schools.

—John Greenleaf Whittier
"The Barefoot Boy"
1855

Boyhood is a summer sun.
—Edgar Allan Poe
"Tamerlane"
1827

There are so many jolly things to do in this world, and it is so hard to decide, since one cannot do them all, that I am sometimes glad I am past my boyhood and no longer have this perplexing problem ahead of me.

—William H. Carruth
Letters to American Boys
1907

A GENTLEMAN

He met his mother on the street;
Off came his little cap.
My door was shut; he waited there
Until I heard his rap.
He took the bundle from my hand,
And when I dropped my pen,
He sprang to pick it up for me—
This gentleman of ten.

—Margaret E. Sangster
Good Manners for all Occasions
1910

No boy who amounts to anything will ever indulge in such expressions as "the old gent," "the governor," and "the old lady," in speaking of his father and mother.

—*Practical Etiquette*
1881

Training is everything. The peach was once a bitter almond; cauliflower is nothing but cabbage with a college education.

—Mark Twain
Pudd'nhead Wilson
1894

The unreasoning eagerness, the motions, the noises which are natural to a thoroughbred pig, should be avoided by a well-bred boy. Who was it that replied, when asked in what he preferred to eat his orange, "In a bath tub"?

—William H. Carruth
Letters to American Boys
1907

When I was a boy of fourteen, my father was so ignorant I could hardly stand to have the old man around. But when I got to be twenty-one, I was astounded at how much the old man had learned in seven years.

—Mark Twain

The
Leisurely Dad

Work consists of whatever a body is *obliged* to do, and **Pl**ay consists of what a body is not obliged to do.

—Mark Twain
Tom Sawyer
1876

I never lost a little fish—yes I am free to say,
It was always the biggest fish I caught that got away.

—Eugene Field
"Our Biggest Fish"
1889

The spirit of good sportsmanship is the gist of a well-bred family.

—Samuel S. Drury
Fathers and Sons
c. 1927

Father, dear Father, come home with me now,
The clock in the belfry strikes one;
You said you were coming right home from the shop
As soon as your day's work was done.

—Henry Clay Work
Come Home, Father
1864

A gentleman should not only know how to fence, to box, to ride, to shoot, to swim, and to play at billiards; he must also know how to dance, to walk, and to carry himself. —*Good Manners*
1870

Father was a tolerant man who excused dull sermons and forgave bad amateur plays—the ministers and actors had done their best, he said—but he asked for perfection in a church or Grange Supper. . . .

When a man forsook his own wife's excellent cookery, changed his clothes, hitched up and drove two miles, and then paid 25 cents for a meal, he had a right to expect a lot.

—C. M. Webster
"The Perfect Church Supper"
1939

The card player who cries when he loses should spend his spare time mowing lawns or shoveling snow instead.

—Margaret Fishback
Safe Conduct
1938

It is unjust to claim the privileges of age, and retain the playthings of childhood.

—Samuel Johnson
The Rambler
September 8, 1750

The doctors say it's good for the circulation to up-end it now and then by tipping back in one's chair and depositing the feet next to the inkwell. That's why men unconsciously assume this delicate balance after lunch.

—Margaret Fishback
Safe Conduct
1938

Father
Knows Best

**My Dear Joe:**

As I looked at the top of my head this evening when I came in from the tennis court I discovered several gray hairs. Therefore I know that I am ripe for giving advice and I shall begin on you.

—William H. Carruth
Letters to American Boys
1907

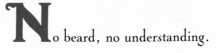

No beard, no understanding.

—German Proverb

It is a waste of breath for the father to order his sons to keep their temper, to behave like gentlemen, or to be good sportsmen, if he does or is himself none of these things.

—Emily Post
Etiquette
1923

Being a good father requires knowing when it is an unkindness to your child to let him do as he pleases if what he wants to do is unreasonable or not conducive to happy family living.

—O. Spurgeon English, M.D., and Constance J. Foster
Fathers Are Parents, Too
c. 1951

My Dear Daughter:

Be very good. Do not bump yourself. Do not eat matches. Do not play with scissors or cats. Do not forget your dad. Sleep when your mother wishes it. Love us both. Try to know how we love you. *That* you will never learn. Goodnight and God keep you, and bless you.

Your Dad

—Letter from Richard Harding Davis
to his daughter
October 24, 1915

Take care that you never spell a word wrong. Always before you write a word, consider how it is spelt, and, if you do not remember it, turn to a dictionary. It produces great praise to a lady to spell well.

—Letter from Thomas Jefferson
to his daughter, Martha
November 28, 1783

It seems fitting that a book about traditions of the past should be decorated with period artwork. In that spirit, the art in *One Swell Dad* has been taken from personal collections of original nineteenth- and early twentieth-century drawings, advertising cards, and other popular paper treasures of the time.

The endpapers and chapter openings contain patterns reproduced from some of our favorite paisleys and foulards.